Jump On, Jump Off!

Written by June Crebbin

Illustrated by Martina Peluso

Collins

There are sights to see
for you and me.

Jump on the bus
it's waiting for us!

See a fleet of ships set sail.
A fish with hair and a bright green tail.

She rests on a rock, and swims in
the deep,

singing sweet songs to lull you to sleep.

Off to the starlight in the dark.
Perch on the moon, see stars spark.

Swing up and down, zoom out of sight, grab a shooting star speeding in the night.

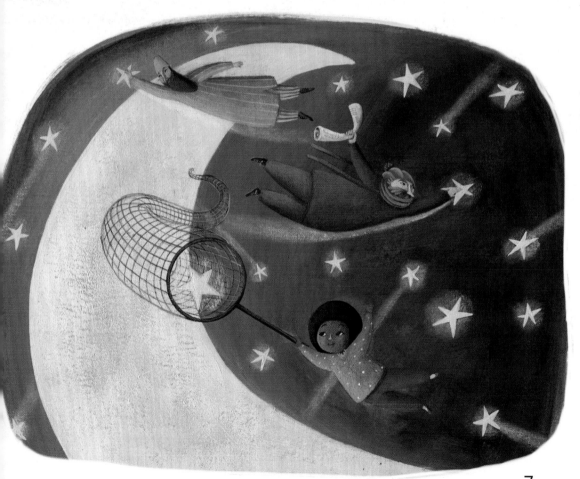

On to a land so damp and still.
Sleet is deep on the brow of a hill.

8

Greet a man in a scarf and hat,
and stop for a sandwich and a chat!

Up to the treetops in a night so black.
Ask an owl for a lift on its back.

Sweep and swoop in darting flight,
get a grip, cling on tight!

Bow to a king in a cloak and crown.
Meet a queen in a long silk gown.

By the light of the sun, the stars and moon,

jump on the bus, we will be back soon!

Jump on the bus!

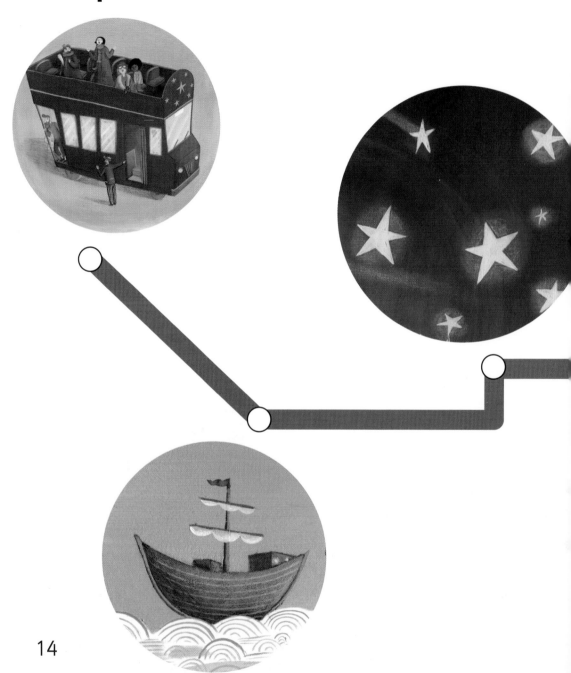

After reading

Letters and Sounds: Phase 4

Word count: 184

Focus on adjacent consonants with long vowel phonemes, e.g. /f/ /l/ /ee/ /t/

Common exception words: to, the, by, are, she, we, me, be, you, so, there, out, ask

Curriculum links: Geography: geographical skills and fieldwork

National Curriculum learning objectives: Spoken language: listen and respond appropriately to adults and their peers; Reading / Word reading: apply phonic knowledge and skills as the route to decode words, read accurately by blending sounds in unfamiliar words containing GPCs that have been taught, read other words of more than one syllable that contain taught GPCs, read aloud accurately books that are consistent with their developing phonic knowledge; Reading / Comprehension: develop pleasure in reading, motivation to read, vocabulary and understanding by discussing word meanings, linking new meanings to those already known

Developing fluency

- Your child may enjoy hearing you read the book. Model reading with lots of expression.
- Now ask your child to read some of the book again, reading with expression themselves.

Phonic practice

- Model sounding out the following word, saying each of the sounds quickly and clearly. Then blend the sounds together

  s/p/ar/k

- Ask your child to say each of the sounds in the following words and then blend them together, one syllable 'chunk' at a time.

  treetops   shooting   speeding   sandwich

- Now ask your child if they can read each of the words without sounding them out.

Extending vocabulary

- Ask your child to spot the synonyms below. Which is the odd one out?

  grip   cling   hold   zoom   (*zoom*)

- On page 11, what is the character doing? What do the words 'sweep and swoop' describe? (*flight*)